Angela
AND THE BABY JESUS

FRANK McCOURT
ILLUSTRATED BY RAÚL COLÓN

SCHOLASTIC INC.
New York Toronto London Auckland Sydney
Mexico City New Delhi Hong Kong Buenos Aires

ISBN-13: 978-0-545-12782-0
ISBN-10: 0-545-12782-3

Text copyright © 2007 by Frank McCourt.
Illustrations copyright © 2007 by Raúl Colón. All rights reserved.
Published by Scholastic Inc., 557 Broadway, New York, NY 10012, by arrangement with Simon & Schuster Books for Young Readers, an imprint of Simon & Schuster Children's Publishing Division. SCHOLASTIC and associated logos are trademarks and/or registered trademarks of Scholastic Inc.

12 11 10 9 8 7 6 5 4 3 2 1   8 9 10 11 12 13/0

Printed in Mexico   49

First Scholastic printing, November 2008

Book design by Lizzy Bromley

The text for this book is set in Old Claude.

The illustrations for this book are rendered with watercolor, colored pencil, and lithograph pencil.

To the memory of my mother, Angela,
who told a story that lodged in my seven-year-old mind
—F. M.

For my dear aunt Carmen
—R. C.

When my mother, Angela,

was six years old, she felt sorry for the Baby Jesus in the Christmas crib at St. Joseph's Church near School House Lane where she lived. She thought the Baby Jesus was cold and wondered why no one had put a blanket over his plump little body. He looked happy enough, smiling up at his mother, the Virgin Mary, and St. Joseph and the three shepherds carrying little lambs all cozy in their fur. Even if he was cold he'd never complain because the Baby Jesus would never want to make his mammy the slightest bit unhappy.

Little Angela wouldn't let it go at that. She was often cold herself, hungry too, but never complained for fear of being told by her mother and brothers and sister to stop the whingeing. (That's what they called whining and complaining in Ireland.) No, she'd have to do something about the poor little Baby Jesus and she wouldn't tell a soul in the world.

A few days before Christmas she hid in a confession booth, the middle part where the priest sits, and peeked out from time to time to see if the church was empty. Old people like Mrs. Reidy and Mr. King knelt in the pews praying, snuffling, and thumping their chests, and Angela wondered why they didn't go home and have a nice cup of tea with lots and lots of sugar. When she let out a little sneeze herself, the old people looked frightened, wondering where that sneeze came from. They whispered to one another there must be a ghost in the church and shuffled away as fast as they could.

Little Angela waited a while till she was sure the church was empty. All she could hear now was the talk of people passing outside and the clop clop of horses on the street.

She thought about what she was going to do, but she knew from lessons in school that stealing is a bad thing and you could be punished. You could be sent to bed without even a cup of tea. Even if you took a penny from your mother's purse you could be punished, so what would be the punishment for stealing the Baby Jesus? Her own mother would surely slap her bottom, but she didn't want to think about that. She had to take care of that poor little Baby Jesus before he turned blue with the cold altogether.

She was surprised at how cold and stiff he was, not soft like the babies in her lane. When she lifted him from the crib, he kept on smiling at her the way he smiled at everyone else, the Virgin Mary, St. Joseph, and the three nice shepherds with their lambs and the Three Wise Kings with all their presents. She felt sorry for them that they wouldn't be able to look at the Baby Jesus anymore, but they didn't seem to mind. Besides, making him warm was the important thing and they'd never begrudge him that.

She had to be careful. She wouldn't want anyone to see her carrying the Baby to her house. She trotted quickly down the aisle and outside where it was now dark. The gaslights flickered along the streets and she could hide and wait in the deep shadows

between. It was cold and people passing by were not in the mood to be looking at a little girl carrying something white in the dark. People wanted to be home sipping a nice hot cup of tea and warming their legs by the fire.

Then she stopped. How was she going to take the Baby Jesus into her house with everyone gawking and wanting to know who was that and what she was doing? She wouldn't go in the front door. There was a lane behind her house where she could carry the Baby over the wall and into her backyard. No, the wall was too high. She could climb over herself, but not with the Baby. She talked to him. "Will you help me, little Baby? Will you help me?"

He did. He told her in her head to throw the Baby over the wall and recover him on the other side. That was hard. She threw and threw and he wouldn't go over till she threw the third time and over he went.

Then the terrible thing happened. When she climbed up and looked into her backyard, there was no sign of him. Now what was she going to do? Where did he go? She was only six, but she knew how serious it was to lose the Baby Jesus. If she didn't find him, he'd be cold and calling for his mother.

Ah, there he was, all white in the dark, lying in the backyard of the blind woman next door, Mrs. Blake.

Now, perched on the wall, she talked to him sternly. Here she was trying to help him and there was no excuse for the way he was behaving, flying around like a bird and landing in a backyard where he wasn't supposed to be. She told him, "Baby Jesus, I have a good mind to leave you there in Mrs. Blake's backyard." But she couldn't. If God ever found out, he'd never let her have a sweet or a bun for a whole week. She told the Baby, "When I throw you over the wall, you're not supposed to land in Mrs. Blake's backyard. You're not to be flying around like an angel."

She climbed down to Mrs. Blake's backyard and picked him up. This time, in one throw, he went over the wall into her own yard and that proved he was paying attention even if he had the same smile. She loved the way his hands and arms still reached out the way they did in the crib. She climbed into her own backyard, told him he was a good Baby for going where he was thrown, and hugged him to warm him up in that cold dark December night.

She nearly died of fright when the back door of her house creaked and out came her brother Pat going to the lavatory. He stopped and stared at her and the Baby, but she didn't mind because he was like a baby himself and often said foolish things even she wouldn't say.

"Is that the Baby Jesus you have there?"

"'Tis."

"He's supposed to be sleeping in his crib abroad in the church an' you have him here in the freezing cold."

"I'm warming him up," she said.

"His mother will be roarin' an' bawlin' when she sees him gone."

"She won't mind. She wants him to be warm, too."

"All right so."

He went into the lavatory and she stepped quietly along the little hall and up the stairs. She stopped at the top when she heard Pat's voice.

"Mammy, Angela do have the Baby Jesus up the stairs."

"Ah, now, Pat, love," said his mother. "You have a great imagination. Sit there an' have your tea."

"She do, Mammy. She have the Baby Jesus above an' he's all white an' shiverin.'"

"All right, Pat. We'll talk to her."

"His mammy will be roarin' an' bawlin.'"

"Don't worry your poor head, Pat."

Little Angela knew she wouldn't be able to keep the Baby in the bed she shared with her sister, Aggie, all night. She'd let him rest there a while, all nice and warm in a blanket, and when it was time to go to sleep, she'd put him under the bed and hope he was comfortable till morning.

Her mother was surprised to see her coming down the stairs at teatime instead of in the front door.

"Was it having a bit of a rest you were?"

"'Twas."

After tea she was allowed to sit by the fire listening to the talk of her family. She always wanted to say something, but she was told she was too young and to shush up. She was only six, so what could she ever say that was important?

Tonight she didn't mind one bit. She had a big secret: Baby Jesus above in the bed nice and warm. It was hard for her to keep that secret, but she could not say a word or they'd all want to see him and play with him like any old doll. She had a doll once which she still cried over when she remembered how her sister, Aggie, pulled its head off and laughed.

Her family laughed again when Pat told them how he'd seen Angela with the Baby Jesus in her arms out in the backyard, but when they laughed, he cried, "She have God in the bed, so she do."

"All right, Pat. All right," his mother said. You could see she wanted to humor him. "We'll all go up and see if the Baby Jesus is in the bed."

Little Angela was terrified there by the fire. What would she do if the family went upstairs and found the Baby Jesus in the bed? Her mother would surely slap her bottom and make her go to sleep without her tea and bread.

She followed her mother and her brother Tom and her sister, Aggie, and her brother Pat, the cause of all the trouble, up the stairs.

It was dark in the room, but still you could see the Baby Jesus in the bed, his head on the pillow, his arms stretched out, though it was almost too dark to see that lovely smile.

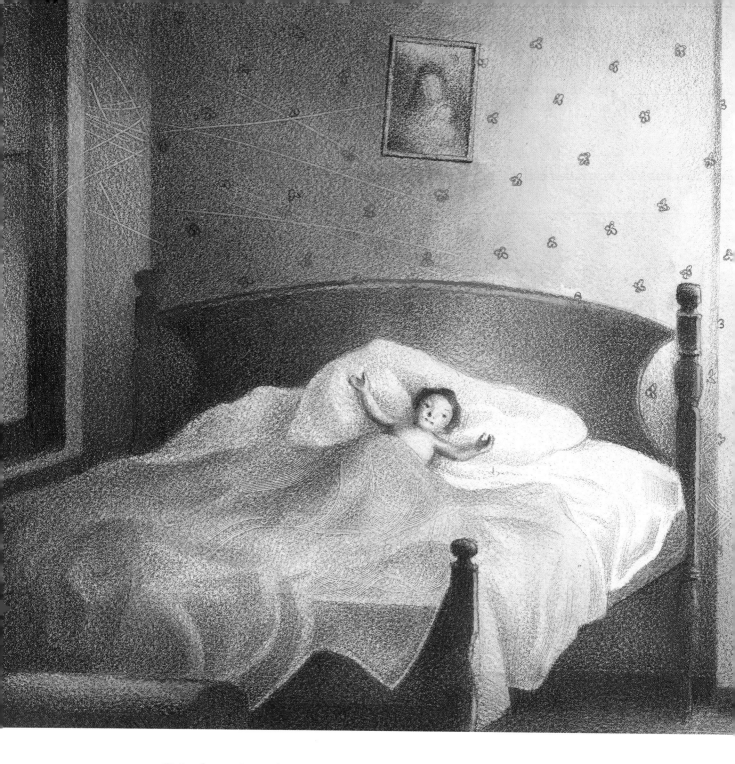

"Mother o' God!" said Little Angela's mother. "Is that the Baby Jesus from St. Joseph's?"

When everyone said "'Tis," Little Angela stayed silent.

Her mother turned to her. "Angela. Did you put that Baby in the bed? Tell the truth because if you tell a lie in the presence of the Baby Jesus it's worse than any sin in the world."

Little Angela wanted to cry, but she didn't. There was something
in her head that told her crying was useless at a time like this.

"I did," she said.

"And why, for the love of God?"

"He was cold in the crib and I wanted to warm him up."

Tom and Aggie laughed and their mother told them be quiet. Little Angela noticed that Pat, the cause of all her trouble, didn't laugh. He said, "I love the Baby Jesus. I'll mind him so he won't be cold."

"Ah, Pat, ah, Pat," said his mother. "Sure, we have to take him back to his poor mother, the Virgin Mary, abroad in the chapel."

Now Pat started to cry. "Please, Mammy, please, Mammy. I'll warm him, and I'll tell his mother we have him safe in the bed."

Little Angela wanted to tell Pat that she was the one who had brought the Baby Jesus here and he had no right to talk about telling the Virgin Mary where her son was.

"Mammy," she said.

"What?" said her mother in a sharp way.

"I want to warm the Baby Jesus. I don't want Pat to be doing anything."

"He's your brother. He loves the Baby Jesus."

"I don't care."

"Anyway, the Baby Jesus has to go back to his mother this very minute."

Now the tears burst from Little Angela's eyes. "Please, please, oh, please."

"Back he goes, Angela, and we'll be lucky if there isn't trouble with the parish priest."

Her mother wrapped the Baby in her black street shawl and they all walked round the corner to return him to his mother and St. Joseph and the shepherds with their nice warm lambs and the Three Wise Kings.

But they were shocked when they found the door of the church locked and shocked even more when the door opened and there was the parish priest, Father Creagh, coming out with a policeman.

"Mother o' God," said Little Angela's mother.

"What's this?" asked the parish priest.

"'Tis the Baby Jesus," said Little Angela's mother.

"I can see that. Here we are the past two hours frantic over that empty crib. Who took him? We have to know and there will be an arrest. Who took him?"

Little Angela tugged at the priest's sleeve. "I did. He was cold in the crib and I took him home to warm him up."

The priest looked at the policeman and the policeman shook his head. "Lord save us," said the policeman. He put his hand on Little Angela's shoulder and said to the priest, "Should we arrest this one, Father. Put her into the Limerick jail?"

"No," said Pat. "No, no, no, no. You won't put my sister in jail. She was only warming the Baby Jesus. You can put me in the Limerick jail."

Poor Pat didn't know what he was talking about, but whatever it was his mother began to cry herself. "Oh, Pat," she said. "Oh, Pat." She had the Baby Jesus in one arm, but she pulled Pat toward her, into her skirt. "Oh, Pat. Oh, Pat. You'd go to jail for your little sister?"

"I would. I would. I love the Baby Jesus and I love my little sister."

The strange thing now was the tears twinkling on the cheeks of the priest in the December moonlight. The policeman coughed and gave his baton a bit of a twirl.

The priest stepped back into the church, cleared his throat, and told everyone to come in out of the cold. "We have to put the Baby back with his poor mother," he told Little Angela.

They walked up the aisle and when they arrived at the altar rail, the priest took the Baby Jesus from Little Angela's mother. He handed the Baby to Little Angela and guided her to the crib.

"You can put him back in his little cradle now," he said in a low gentle way.

"But he'll be cold," said Little Angela.

"Ah, no," said Father Creagh. "When we're not here, his mother, Our Lady, makes sure he's nice and warm."

"Are you sure?"

"I am."

When she put the Baby Jesus back in the crib, he smiled the way he always did and held out his arms to the world.